DRAGON

WAYNE ANDERSON

GREEN TIGER PRESS
Published by Simon & Schuster
New York London Toronto Sydney Tokyo Singapore

O NE morning, something precious dropped from the sky. A mother screamed out for help, but it was too late. It fell down, down, and lost itself in the deep, dark ocean.

The precious thing lay on the ocean floor. The water rocked it, and the quiet voices of the fishes comforted it and told it to be patient.

When the time was right, a tiny crack appeared which spread all around until the precious thing broke clean in two.

A newborn creature looked out at the watery world. And as all new creatures do, he called out for his mother. No answer came. Only the welcoming murmurs of the fishes who had never seen a creature born from such an egg.

"Where is my mother?" asked the creature. "And what am I?" The fishes sighed. "We're not sure," they said. "But perhaps you are a fish for you have scales and fins, like us."

The fishes felt sorry for the poor motherless creature, so they built him a house and fed him on morsels of weed and shell.

Soon the creature began to grow. He grew and grew until the shell house was too small to hold him. The fins on his back grew into tiny wings and he felt a great power stir in his veins.

"I am not a fish," he said. "I must find my own kind and my mother who will love me."

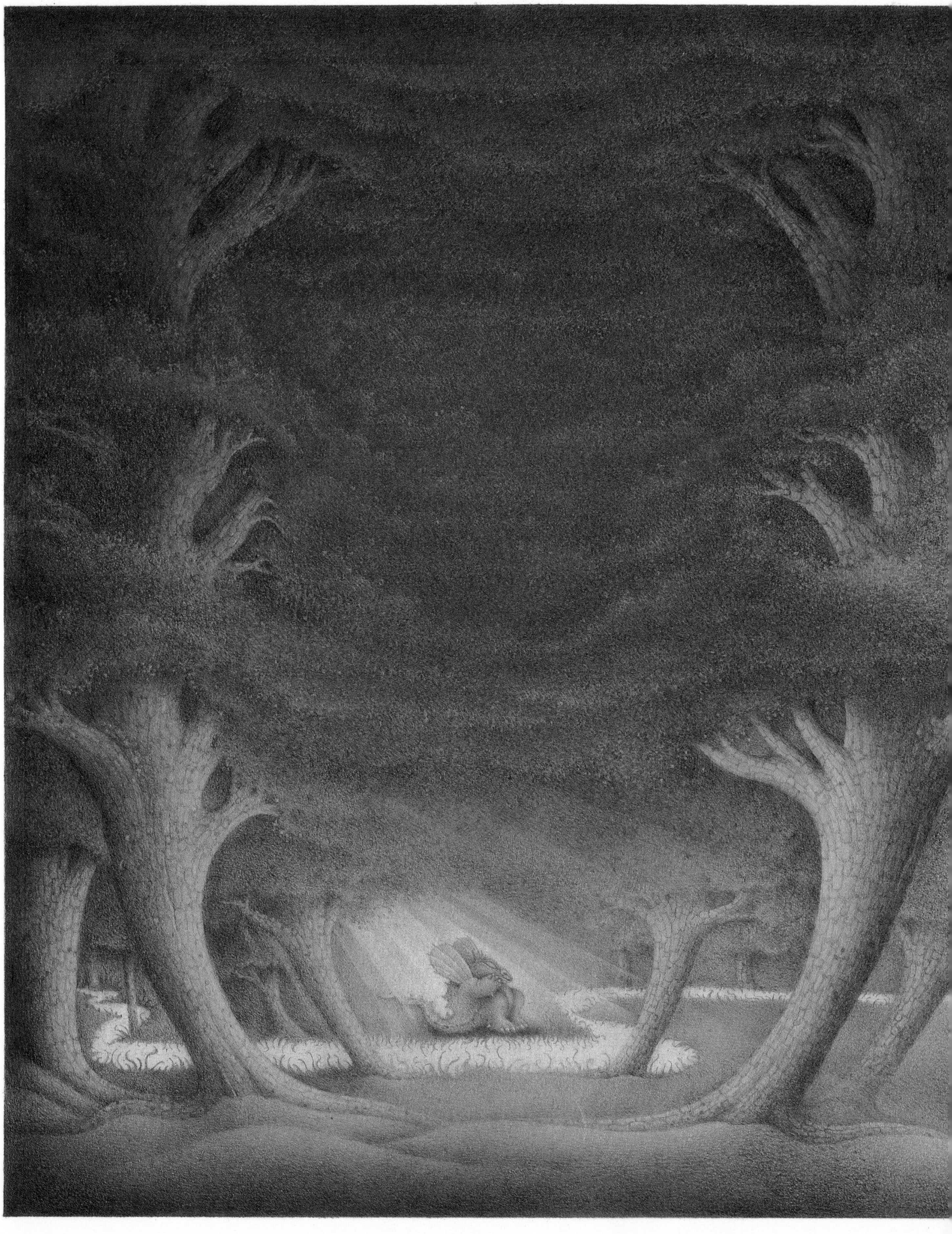

So he swam to the surface of the water where the bright light of the sun warmed his flesh and lifted his spirit. "This must be my home," he said. He swam to the shore and waited for his mother to come to him. "This is a sad, empty place," he said to himself.

Just then there was a loud buzzing as a dragonfly flew by.

"Where is my mother?" asked the creature. "And what am I?"

"I'm not sure," said the dragonfly, "but you have wings, so perhaps you are an insect like me. Let's see if you can fly." The dragonfly spread its wings and flew up into the sky. The small creature tried to copy this but fell and hurt himself.

"Your wings are too new," said the dragonfly. "You will have to practice."

The creature practiced. Day turned into night and night into day. Finally, he took off with a great whoosh. Up and up he went. And up higher still. "I am not a dragonfly," he said. "No insect ever flew as high as this. I must fly on and find my own kind and my mother who will love me."

Suddenly the wind grew fierce, and a flock of birds on their winter flight surrounded the young creature. They squawked and screeched with surprise to see such a strange animal so high up in the sky.

"Where is my mother?" asked the creature. "And what am I?"

"We're not sure," they sang. "But perhaps you are a bird like us, for your wings are strong enough to carry you up to the clouds. Come with us to Africa where the sun is warm and the food is plentiful."

When they arrived, the birds built their nests and settled to roost. As soon as the sun rose they began to sing. The creature joined in, but his voice was so harsh and loud that it traveled to the very roots of the trees and shook the earth. Smoke came on his breath. The animals hid away in fright.

"He is not a bird," they said. "His voice is like thunder and he has scales on his greeny skin. Look how smoke floats on his breath. Off with you!" they cried, and the poor motherless creature slunk away to continue his search.

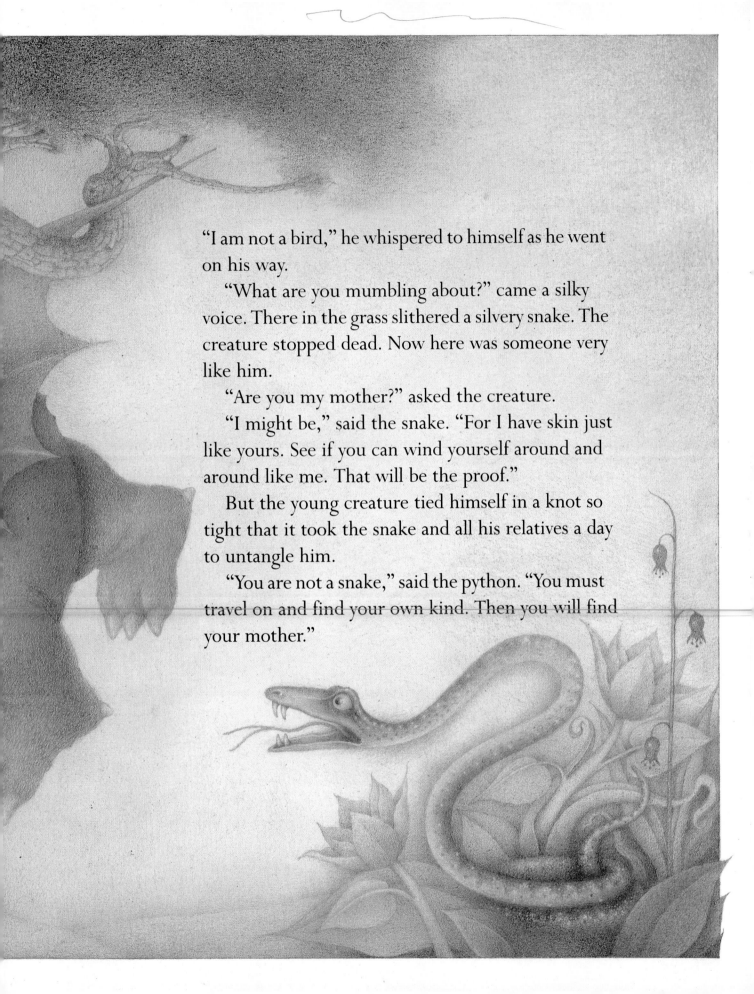

"I am not a bird," he whispered to himself as he went on his way.

"What are you mumbling about?" came a silky voice. There in the grass slithered a silvery snake. The creature stopped dead. Now here was someone very like him.

"Are you my mother?" asked the creature.

"I might be," said the snake. "For I have skin just like yours. See if you can wind yourself around and around like me. That will be the proof."

But the young creature tied himself in a knot so tight that it took the snake and all his relatives a day to untangle him.

"You are not a snake," said the python. "You must travel on and find your own kind. Then you will find your mother."

In the swampy marshlands the creature sat down to rest.

"I am not a fish. I am not an insect. I am not a bird. I am not a snake," he sang to himself.

"No, my sweet. You are a CROCODILE!" came a raspy voice, "and I am your mother. Come here so I may see you clearly."

"Mother?" said the creature. And he looked into the pale yellow eyes and saw his own reflection. "It is true, I am like you," he said.

"We both have scaly green skin and sharp pointed claws," said the crocodile, "and your teeth are chiseled and sharp, just like mine. Come closer and I'll show you."

The crocodile opened its cavernous mouth and the creature saw his fate within.

"No, I am NOT a crocodile," he said. And swiftly he spread his wings and shot into the sky. "I am *not* a crocodile. I am *not* a crocodile," he cried.

Now the creature was growing up, and he began to discover the true power of his wings. He flew swifter than an eagle, fast and long. And as time passed, the sun sank low and the wind grew cold and the country below changed from a golden yellow to an icy gray. He flew over forests, fields and a vast sea where there was nothing but blue.

The wind turned cold and carried him along on its icy breath.

"MOTHER!" screeched the creature, and the echo, like a pain of longing, bounced around the sky. There was no answer. Eventually the creature grew tired, but not until he had flown a thousand miles. Then he saw a thin line of smoke trailing from a strange white animal. He remembered the smoke he had made in the jungle and turned his way earthwards. "Perhaps my mother is here," he said.

As he approached, he made out a shape as large as himself, with big yellow eyes.

He glided down and looked in the eye of the silent, still animal. And inside the eye was light. And inside the light there was a small creature wrapped up in softness.

"You are not like me," said the creature as quietly as he could, for he didn't want to frighten the little thing. "But can you help me? Where is my mother? And what am I?"

The human child looked up in wonder. He was not frightened for he knew magic from his storybooks. He looked at his book and he looked at the face at the window. "You are a wonderful thing, and I am reading about you in this book." He held the picture to the window so the creature could look at the image of himself.

"I have discovered my own kind," the creature cried joyfully. "But I need my mother. Can you tell me where she is?"

The child knew what it was to need your mother. So he put on his scarf and his coat, went outside and climbed upon the dragon's back. "I will take you home," he said. "And we will take this book as a guide, for there's a map inside."

"It says here that we must go northwards, to the very edge of the earth where the rivers run into a great lake, and where magic is at its strongest," said the boy.

And as they flew, the boy studied the map and watched carefully the changing landscape below. And all the time it grew colder and colder, and the creature's wings grew heavier and heavier, until finally they were forced to land so the creature could take some rest. They lay down to sleep and the creature raised his belly so the little child could crawl under to keep warm.

But the cold finds its true strength in the night. In the morning the two young creatures woke to find themselves frozen to the ground.

"Oh," cried the creature. "We are trapped here. We will die and I will never know my mother's love."

"Wait," said the boy, looking in the book. "It says here you can make fire."

The creature blew and felt fire on his breath. Huge flames of red and orange shot from his mouth. They lit up the sky, they warmed the icy cage and melted it into the snow.

Up they flew again, across the great lake and through the frozen landscape to the very edge of the world.

"There is your home," said the boy, pointing to a high mountain. And from it appeared a host of magnificent winged cratures, all with green scaly skin and sharp pointed teeth. Then one, bigger than the rest, rose up from the crowd and cried with joy, "My child!"

And the young creature knew that voice from long ago, from a time before his search had begun, before his life underwater, a time when he was just a warm egg. Gently lowering the boy onto the snow, he flew to his mother. She enveloped him in her great wings and, holding him close, named him: Dragon.

For Jenny, the Dragon Lady

GREEN TIGER PRESS

Simon & Schuster Building, Rockefeller Center

1230 Avenue of the Americas, New York, New York 10020

Copyright © 1992 by Wayne Anderson

Originally published in Great Britain by Hutchinson Children's Books.

GREEN TIGER PRESS is an imprint of Simon & Schuster.

Manufactured in Hong Kong.

10 9 8 7 6 5 4 3 2 1

Library of Congress Cataloging-in-Publication Data

Anderson, Wayne. Dragon / by Wayne Anderson. p. cm.

Summary: After hatching from an egg that fell into the sea,

a creature that shares features with a fish, an insect,

a bird, and a snake — but is not any of these — sets off

to find its own kind and its mother.

[1. Dragons — Fiction. 2. Identity — Fiction. 3. Fantasy.]

I. Title. PZ7.A556Dr 1992 [E] — dc20 91-47906 CIP

ISBN: 0-671-78397-1